DISNEY
THE
LITTLE
MERMAID

THIS IS ARIEL

Written by Colin Hosten
Illustrated by the Disney Storybook Art Team

Screenplay by David Magee
Based on Disney's *The Little Mermaid*

DISNEY PRESS
LOS ANGELES • NEW YORK

This is Ariel.

She is a mermaid!

Ariel lives under the sea.
The sea is full of mermaids
and other sea creatures!

This is Ariel's father, King Triton.

He is a king.

That makes Ariel a princess!

Ariel is from a big family.
She has six sisters!

Each has her own
unique personality.

This is Ariel's best friend, Flounder.
Ariel enjoys swimming
and exploring with him.

They visit shipwrecks together, but they must keep an eye out for sharks!

Ariel is very curious about
the world of humans.

She collects all kinds of objects
and treasures.
She keeps them safe in her grotto.

This is Scuttle. She is an expert on human objects!

Ariel shares what she finds
with Scuttle.

But sometimes Ariel wishes
for something more
than just human objects.

Perhaps a new adventure
with humans—on the surface!

This is Prince Eric.
He lives in a castle on land.
But he enjoys sailing the sea.
He wants to go on
a new adventure, too.

If only Ariel could be
part of Eric's world!
They could go on
adventures together.

Ariel saves Eric from a storm.
She sings to him.

When he wakes up,
he remembers her beautiful voice.

This is Sebastian.
He doesn't understand why
Ariel would want to go on land.

He believes they have everything they could ever need under the sea!

This is Ursula, the sea witch.
She is always up to some trick.

Ursula uses her magic
to transform Ariel into a human!

Now Ariel can be with Eric
on the surface.

There are so many new things to learn.

There are new objects to play with!

There are new places to explore!

Ariel even learns to drive a carriage.
Eric is only a little afraid.

She spots a dinglehopper
at the market. Fortunately,
she knows just how to use it!

The human world is full of
new adventures . . .

. . . like boat rides through lagoons.

Together, Ariel and Eric
have much more to explore.